Travels with Dad

by Coco Relf
illustrated by Barry Gott

Harcourt

Orlando   Boston   Dallas   Chicago   San Diego

Visit *The Learning Site!*

www.harcourtschool.com

Grace, Jack, and their father were loading their luggage into the car. "Did you bring the map?" asked Grace.

"Map?" said their father, waving his hand. "I don't need a map to find Aunt Coco's house." Grace and Jack looked at each other and sighed.

"Dad, Aunt Coco moved," said Jack.

"Piece of cake," said his father. "We have a sturdy car, and I have this gift for finding my way around. Just sit back and listen to a cassette. I'll do the rest."

That, thought Grace, *is what we're afraid of*. Every time Dad took Jack and Grace to visit relatives, they got lost. Once they drove to the wrong state. Another time, they ended up in the middle of a parade.

About two hours into the trip, Dad
stopped the car. He looked puzzled. "I
thought we were near the highway," he
muttered. Then he pointed through the
trees and said in a cheery voice, "Well,
look over there!"

Jack and Grace were amazed to see steam rising from the ground! "What is that, Dad?" they asked.

"It's a hot spring," he told them. "Water comes out of the earth warm here. Let's get our swimsuits. This could be fun!" He grabbed his camera and jumped out.

Grace and Jack looked at each other.
Then they grabbed their swimsuits.

The spring had formed a pool of
steamy water. Dad dipped in a toe to
check how hot it was. "The water's fine!"
he said. "In we go!"

An hour later, they were back in the
car, dried off, and feeling warm and clean.
Dad drove on, but soon he stopped the
car again. "Hmmm," he said, frowning.
Then he smiled and pointed. "Look
over there!"

"Look at that field of flowers!" he said. "How about a picnic? I have everything we need."

He opened the trunk and took out a sturdy picnic basket. Then off they went together through the wildflowers.

An hour later, they were back in the car.
Dad had taken lots of pictures. Grace and
Jack had picked a bunch of wildflowers
for Aunt Coco. Grace was smelling the
flowers when Dad stopped the car again.

"Dad. Are you lost again?" Jack asked.
"Lost?" their father asked, sounding
surprised. "Of course not! I just stopped
because—well, look at that!" He pointed.

There, way off in the trees, was a
quiet pond. Something was moving
around on the water.

Dad picked up his camera again.
"Come on, kids!" he said. Then he was
out of the car, walking toward the pond.

Grace and Jack ran after him. As they got close to the pond, a large white bird swooped down. It joined a dozen companions that were gliding over the smooth water.

"Swans!" Jack said. The swans turned their graceful necks to look at him.

"Dad," Grace said softly, "they're beautiful!" The swans left a slight ripple as they moved. The sun was setting, and Grace could see the swans reflected in the water. She and Jack stood silently watching while Dad took pictures.

When the sun went down, Grace, Jack and their dad got back into the car. They were quiet, thinking about all they had seen. They were glad they would have lots of pictures as souvenirs of this trip.

In a few minutes, Dad stopped the car once more. "We're there!" he said happily.

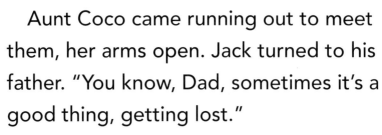

Aunt Coco came running out to meet them, her arms open. Jack turned to his father. "You know, Dad, sometimes it's a good thing, getting lost."

"I don't call it getting lost," his father said, smiling at him. "I call it adventure!"